WHEN IMAGINATION TALKS TO YOU!

I DREAM TO BE

WRITTEN BY

REBECCA T. CLARK

ILLUSTRATIONS BY CHRIS HOUSE

Cover and illustrations. Chris House Studio Painted Blade, LLC

Printed in the United States of America – St. Louis, Missouri

First Printing, 2017

Library of Congress Control Number- 2017906154

ISBN-10: 0-692-93977-6
ISBN-13: 978-0-692-93977-2

Be Heard Publishing, LLC

www.wittykidsclub.com
wittykidsbook@gmail.com

Hi, my name is Jersey! I'm a witty kid. I am clever. I am creative. I like to write, draw, play sports, and I'm a straight A student in school. I like to make people laugh and smile. I like to learn and come up with ideas. One more thing about me is that I love to dream!

When I dream, I wonder what it takes to make the dream come true. I dream at all times of the day. Sometimes I dream on the playground, in the car, at the store, and at night during bedtime.

This book is to all the young readers:
"The world wants to see your vision. The world wants to hear your ideas. The world wants to know your inspiration. Use your imagination to go places beyond your wildest dreams. The world is so big and we need all of you. Always see beauty in the dark and the light, for your passions can come from the smallest places."

- Witty Kids

My friends tell me that I have a big imagination. Sometimes, I help them create new ideas for school projects. One day, I told my mom that I wanted to invent something when I grow up. I told her that I want to invent a garbage truck that looks like a vacuum. Can you imagine that?

From that day on, my mom gave me the idea to start writing down my dreams. She told me to use my imagination and write about my ideas, write stories, and write words so that I never forget.

Well, I took her advice and started writing in my journal every night.

4

I must admit, I am a little nervous about sharing my dreams since this is my first time writing about my ideas.

Writing should be easy, so I will start by writing what is on my mind.

My goal is to inspire all my friends, so that they can do it too!

So, come on and....

I dream to be an astronaut:
If this dream came true, I would imagine I could fly into space inside a spaceship and put on a really cool space suit. I would imagine I learn all about planets, space, and gravity. I wonder if I could design my own space suit, and use lots of neon colors, patches, and buttons.

I would imagine I could get to explore views of the universe to help researchers build better technology.

As an astronaut, I would be reaching for the stars!

8

I dream to be an engineer:
If this dream came true, I would imagine I could build ideas and new products. I would imagine that math would be my favorite subject. I would question how things work and how they are created.

I would learn about different systems using a computer and cool tools. I would use my imagination to come up with inventions that have never been created before.

As an engineer, I would be full of ideas!

10

I dream to be a chef:

If this dream came true, I would imagine that I would love to cook. I would make meals inside a kitchen or a restaurant. I would imagine that I would like the smell and taste of different types of food. I would learn how to mix spices together to make the perfect dish.

I would create recipes that people would love to eat. I would use fresh ingredients and measure everything properly. As a specialty, I would cook my favorite vegetables. Yummy!

As a chef, I would be a treat!

11

12

I dream to be an artist:

If this dream came true, I would imagine I would wear a painter's hat that is three times larger than my head. I would imagine that I would have a palette, a blank canvas, and an easel to draw my favorite pictures. I would learn how to use different techniques on sketching and drawing.

I would use my sharp pencils and brushes to create my best designs. I would keep all my favorite drawings in a portfolio to show off my work.

As an artist, I would be a piece of work!

I dream to be a fashion designer:
If this dream came true, I would imagine I would have my own style. I would learn how to design and make clothes. I would use my creativity to design outfits, pillows, shoes, and all kinds of fun things.

I would imagine I would learn about fabrics, patterns, and different types of materials, so that I can make a variety of products.

As a fashion designer, I would be very trendy!

I dream to be a director:
If this dream came true, I would imagine I would direct the making of plays and movies. I would imagine that I would learn how to select a cast from start to finish of the film. I would learn about screens and editing techniques.

I imagine that after each scene I would say, "Cut!"
I imagine that I would work with a team to create a funny movie.

As a director, I would be good at giving directions!

18

I dream to be a veterinarian.
If this dream came true, I would imagine that I love animals. I would imagine that I would take care of all animals, even when they are sick. I would also take care of the furry rabbits and small puppies when they need vaccinations and bandages for their wounds.

I would imagine I would help them to be healthy creatures. I would make sure pets that are big or small would be treated the same.

As a veterinarian, I would be a pet doctor!

20

I dream to be an author:

If this dream came true, I would imagine I love to write. I would love to create stories that turn into books. I would use my imagination to write about stories that have happened or write about ideas that I wish came true.

I would imagine that I would love to write novels or poems to express my creativity. I would use my imagination to give the characters cool names.

As an author, I would be a great storyteller!

22

Now that my thoughts are ending, your dreams are just beginning. I am absolutely convinced that by opening my journal of dreams, you will gain the hope and confidence you need to dream big too.

My advice is to use your imagination and write your own ideas everyday. Start with an idea, and then think about what it will take to make that dream come true. I want all my friends to join me on this journey!

Let's use our clever personalities to create inspiration.

What do you dream to be?

construction worker

fire fighter

doctor

carpenter

gymnast

astronaut

programmer

coach

teacher

actress

doctor veterinarian

author dentist

police officer

basketball player

artist

athlete

dream

baseball player

lawyer

pilot musician + chef

film director

hairstylist

engineer

football player

fashion designer

marine

photographer

electrician

video gamer

26